Sparkly Sophie and the Sparkle Princess Birthday Party

written by: Kristin Evans

illustrated by: Joan Coleman

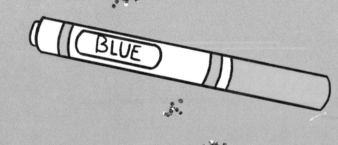

BLUE

GREEN

This Book Belongs To:

_____

Sparkly Sophie and the Sparkle Princess Birthday Party

written by: Kristin Evans

illustrated by: Joan Coleman

Kristin dedicates this book:
To my Mom and Dad - Thank you for making me feel loved and celebrated from the very start.
To my sister and brother - Thank you for always supporting me ... and my parties.
To Spencer - Thank you for making me feel like a sparkly princess every day.
To all the little princes and princesses I've come to know - Thank you for inspiring me with your love and joy for life!
I appreciate and love you all!

Joan dedicates this book to:
To my best friend, my husband Andrew.

Sparkly Sophie and the Sparkle Princess Birthday Party

Written by Kristin Evans and Illustrated by Joan Coleman.

Sophie loved to plan parties. No matter what the holiday, occasion, or day of the year, she could plan a party for it. There was **one** party that Sophie absolutely loved to plan the most.

She thought of this party all year long.
She dreamed of this party.
She made countdown charts to this party.
It was …

♡♡ Very Important
Party Planning Meeting
where: dining room
when: Saturday at 4:00pm
why: party planning

BLUE

from:
Sophie

to: Mom and Dad

Crafting

Dear Mom and Dad,
I'm excited to see you
at the party planning
meeting tonight!
Love,
Sophie

When the countdown chart read
"ONLY 100 days left until the big day,"
Sophie gathered her official party planning
committee - **Mom and Dad** - for a
special meeting.

PINK

GREEN

Countdown

92
93
94 83 82
95 84 73
96 85 74 63
97 86 75 64
98 87 76 65 54 53
99 88 77 66 55 44 43
100 89 78 67 56 45 34 33
90 79 68 57 46 35 24 23
80 69 58 47 36 25 14
70 59 48 37
60

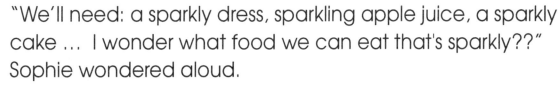

"We'll need: a sparkly dress, sparkling apple juice, a sparkly cake … I wonder what food we can eat that's sparkly??" Sophie wondered aloud.

"Mom? Dad?" Sophie asked. "Can we put sparkles on pepperoni pizza this year?"

Sophie's Mom and Dad looked at each other with a smile. Although no one loved planning this party more than Sophie, they truly enjoyed seeing the thrill and delight it brought to their daughter every year.

Sophie continued. "I think the girls are going to **LOVE** dressing up as princesses. Right?" Suddenly Sophie stopped. Her eyes widened and started to sparkle a little more than usual.

"Are you okay, Sweetie?" her Dad asked. "I know we're talking about sparkles, but the sparkle in your eyes looks a lot like tears."

Sophie tried to hold it together. She loved sparkles **SO** much that if her tears made her sparkle even more, it couldn't be all that bad. But the sad feeling she felt was just too much to keep inside.

"What if no one likes my Sparkle Princess Party games?!?!"
Sophie exclaimed as the sparkles in her eyes burst into tears.

Sophie felt that over the years she had perfected the Sparkle Princess Birthday Parties that she enjoyed every year with her friends.

The problem was that Sophie and her family had just moved, so she had to start all over again in a new town, at a new school, with new friends.

None of her new friends had ever been to one of her Sparkle Princess Birthday Parties before.

Sophie looked at her Mom. "Will they like playing **Crowning Castle Wall** where we jump over the blocks as they are stacked higher and higher?"

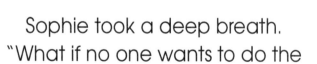

"Dad, what if they don't like playing **Daring Diamond** where we throw the jewels into the treasure chest?!"

Sophie took a deep breath. "What if no one wants to do the **Princess Portraits** where we make dazzling drawings of each other?!?!"

"This could be the **worst** Princess Party in the history of my life!!!!"

"I'm sorry you're feeling so stressed out about your party," Sophie's Mom said as she brought Sophie onto her lap for a cuddle. "Do you remember anyone who hasn't enjoyed playing Crowning Castle Wall?"

Sophie thought for a moment.
"No ..." she replied.

"Do you know anyone who didn't like protecting jewels in Daring Diamond?" her Dad asked.

"Hmm ..." Sophie pondered.
"I don't think so."

"And who hasn't enjoyed Princess Portraits?" her Mom wondered.

Sophie thought and thought.
"I can't think of anyone."

"Well then, let's focus on getting ready for the party and how we can help make sure your new friends feel like princesses while they're here," Sophie's Mom reassured.

After a family hug, Sophie felt much better.

Over the next few weeks Sophie tried not to worry about the party. While she was finalizing the party plans one day, she had a fabulous thought.

She told her Mom, "Maybe I'll make a sparkly **tiara** for each of my friends to wear in case they don't have one of their own!"

Her Mom agreed that this was a wonderful idea, but reminded Sophie it would take a lot work.

Sophie's family had a rule about parties: if you wanted to ask a few of the girls in your class, you had to ask ALL of the girls in the class so no one would feel left out.

Sophie loved this rule!

She remembered the feeling of not being invited and did not want anyone to feel that way with her parties.

50
Days Left:

Sophie started working hard on the special party favors she wanted to give to her friends. After days and hours of measuring, cutting, gluing, and coloring, Sophie finished making the sparkly, jeweled tiaras for her party guests.

Using:

1 pair of scissors
2 packages of stick-on jewels
3 colors of construction paper
lots and lots of sparkles

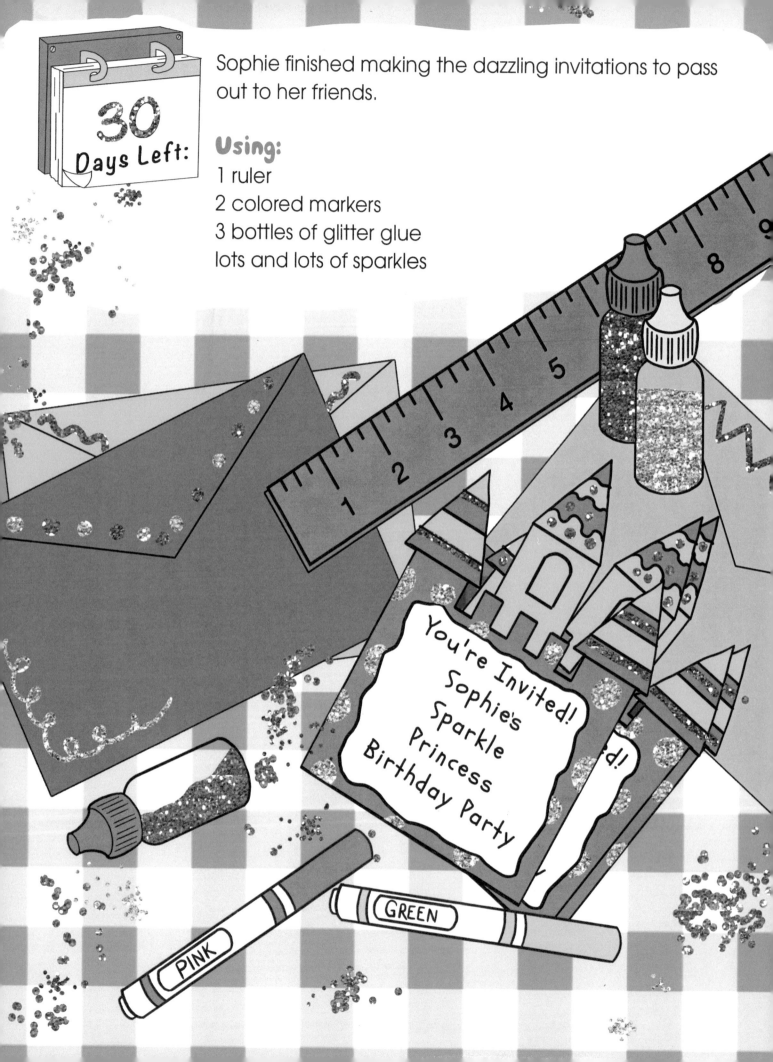

Sophie finished making the dazzling invitations to pass out to her friends.

Using:
1 ruler
2 colored markers
3 bottles of glitter glue
lots and lots of sparkles

30 Days Left:

You're Invited!
Sophie's
Sparkle
Princess
Birthday Party

PINK

GREEN

20 Days Left:

It was finally time to pass out the invitations! Sophie's Mom let her wear her second favorite sparkly dress to school that day (of course, she was saving her **ABSOLUTE** favorite sparkly dress for the party).

She wanted to look extra **sparkly** as she invited her classmates to the big day!

At recess Sophie asked the girls in her class to meet her at the **playground castle.** It was the perfect place to invite her special guests.

"Hi everyone! In 20 days I'm having a Sparkle Princess Birthday Party and I'd love for you all to come!"

Samantha stopped Sophie. "You're inviting all of us?" "Yes!" Sophie exclaimed. All the girls perked up. This was a new idea for the girls in the class. They had never **ALL** been invited before! As Sophie passed out the invitations, she felt relieved when she saw the girls' smiles.

"Maybe this **WILL** be a success after all!" Sophie thought.

With a new confidence, Sophie continued. "It is a **princess** party so please come wearing your favorite princess dress. We're going to play princess games, eat lots of pizza, and, of course, there will be **sparkles galore!** I hope to see you all there!"

As the girls walked off to class, Sophie noticed that Samantha stayed back.

"I don't think I can come to your party," Samantha said sadly.
"I don't have a princess dress to wear."

"Oh!" Sophie quickly replied.
"If you **WANT** to come to my party,
you can borrow one of my princess dresses!
I really hope you can come!"

Before Samantha could answer, the bell rang and they hurried off to class.

10 Days Left:

Sophie finished preparing the props for all of the princess party games.

Crowning Castle Wall:
5 tiny boxes for stacking
4 small boxes for stacking
3 medium boxes for stacking
2 big boxes for stacking
1 really big box for stacking

Dazzling Diamond:
4 tennis balls
3 small playground balls
2 balloons
1 basket

Pretty Princess Portraits:
10 sheets of paper
10 colored pencils
1 easel

2 Days Left:

Sophie and her Mom went to the store to get the party food. They needed veggies for snacking, sparkling apple juice and the ingredients for pizza and cake!

Snacks:
baby carrots
celery
cherry tomatoes

Pizza:
flour
yeast
pizza sauce
cheese
pepperoni

Cake:
flour
sugar
butter
eggs
vanilla

Frosting:
powdered sugar
butter
milk
sparkly sprinkles

1 Day Left:

Sophie went over the party program:

Sparkly dress? Check!
Sparkly tiaras? Check!
Sparkly sprinkles for cake? Check!
Sparkling apple juice? Check!
Sparkly party props for games? Check!
Sparkly pizza?

Well … no sparkles on the pizza this year, but the yummy, glistening, melted cheese would do!

That last day before the party felt like a whole year to Sophie. **"Would it ever be tomorrow??"** she wondered.

Days Left: 0

After 365 long days of waiting, her birthday party was finally here!!

Sophie woke up extra early so she could take her time getting ready. She put on her favorite sparkly princess dress and her sparkly chapstick. Her Mom gave her a royal hair style and placed a tiara on the top of Sophie's head.

"I'm so excited to celebrate **YOU** today!" her Mom said as she hugged her little princess. "I'm really proud of how hard you've worked to prepare for the party. I think it's going to be a royal blast!"

Sophie's smile beamed. She just loved her Mom … and her hugs.

Samantha came to the party a little early to borrow a dress from Sophie. Sophie was delighted. "I'm so glad you decided to come!! I have the **PERFECT** dress for you! It will look so great on you and will really bring out the sparkle in your eyes!" Sophie exclaimed as they raced off to her room.

Soon the rest of her friends began to arrive and Sophie was thrilled to see all the girls in their dazzling princess outfits. "This is such a great start!" she thought.

Once Sophie greeted all of her friends, it was time for the festivities to begin! She gathered everyone in a circle and took a deep breath.

"Princesses!" Sophie announced. "Today we must jump over the **Captivating Castle Wall!** We will keep our jewels safe by hiding them in our treasure chest in **Daring Diamond.** We will admire each other's loveliness as we draw each other's **Princess Portraits,** and then celebrate the day with a royal feast."

"Princesses, are you ready?!"

"**YEEEEEEEEEESSSSSSSS!!**"
they all screamed and raced out to the backyard.

"Oh, Mom," Sophie exclaimed, "this is already going better than I'd hoped!"

The girls had a terrific time all afternoon as they jumped over castles, protected jewels in their treasure chest and drew portraits of each other

At the end of the party,
  after the games,
    after the portraits,
      after the girls were finished feasting on pepperoni pizza,
        and after they delighted in the delicious sparkly cake,
Sophie took a moment to address her friends.

"I had **so much fun** being princesses with you today! Not only do you all look simply stunning and oh-so-sparkly, but I'm so happy you're all my friends. Thank you for coming to my party and making me feel so special! You will **always** be royal, sparkly princesses to me!"

With that, her Mom and Dad crowned each princess with her very own sparkly tiara that Sophie had made. All the girls beamed with pride.

As Sophie said goodbye to her friends, Samantha stopped in the doorway.

"You know," she said, "usually at our parties we don't have games like this, but it was really **so much fun.** Thank you for sharing your pretty dress with me. And it was cool you invited us. **ALL** of us." Samantha smiled.
"I hope you have a party again next year! I can't wait!" she said as she left with her Mom.

As Sophie got ready for bed that night, she couldn't stop smiling or talking about the party. "It made me feel so special that my new friends came today and had fun playing my princess party games with me," she said as she got into her bed. "You know," Sophie said to her parents, "I think that was the **best** Sparkle Princess Party yet!" Her parents smiled.

As they turned out the light, Sophie said, "I'm so glad my next party is only 365 days away!" And with that sparkly, warming thought, and with a little sparkle left on her cheek, Sophie fell fast asleep.

About the Author:

Kristin Evans' family moved a lot while she was growing up, so she under- stands the feeling of starting over with new friends. She hopes to inspire kids to be confident, kind, creative, fun, inclusive with others, AND to share their own sparkle wherever they go!

For more on all things Sparkly Sophie go to www. SparklySophie.com!

About the Artist:

Joan Coleman is an illustrator and designer specializing in children's artwork, fashion and home decor. She hopes to inspire all young readers to be their sparkly selves!

Feel free to visit Joan at: www.InkWonderland.com

Joan's dog Lucy

Kristin's dog Daisy

Made in the USA
San Bernardino, CA
09 June 2018